Dear Parent:
Your child's love of reading starts here!

Every child learns to read in a different way and at his or her own speed. Some go back and forth between reading levels and read favorite books again and again. Others read through each level in order. You can help your young reader improve and become more confident by encouraging his or her own interests and abilities. From books your child reads with you to the first books he or she reads alone, there are I Can Read Books for every stage of reading:

SHARED READING
Basic language, word repetition, and whimsical illustrations, ideal for sharing with your emergent reader

BEGINNING READING
Short sentences, familiar words, and simple concepts for children eager to read on their own

READING WITH HELP
Engaging stories, longer sentences, and language play for developing readers

READING ALONE
Complex plots, challenging vocabulary, and high-interest topics for the independent reader

ADVANCED READING
Short paragraphs, chapters, and exciting themes for the perfect bridge to chapter books

I Can Read Books have introduced children to the joy of reading since 1957. Featuring award-winning authors and illustrators and a fabulous cast of beloved characters, I Can Read Books set the standard for beginning readers.

A lifetime of discovery begins with the magical words "I Can Read!"

Visit www.icanread.com for information
on enriching your child's reading experience.

I Can Read Book® is a trademark of HarperCollins Publishers.

Batman versus the Riddler
Copyright © 2014 DC Comics.
BATMAN and all related characters and elements are trademarks of and © DC Comics.
(s14)

HARP30377

Library of Congress catalog card number: 2013950298
ISBN 978-0-06-221008-1

Book design by Joe Merkel

19 20 21 22   LSCC   10 9   ❖   First Edition

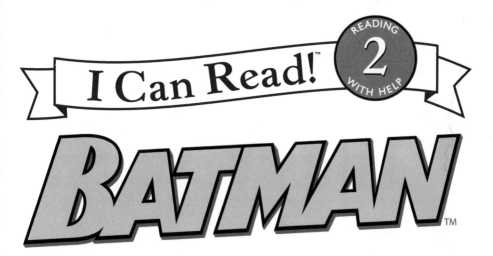

Batman versus the Riddler

by Donald Lemke

pictures by Steven E. Gordon

colors by Eric A. Gordon

BATMAN created by Bob Kane

HARPER
An Imprint of HarperCollinsPublishers

BRUCE WAYNE

Bruce is a rich businessman. Orphaned as a child, he trained his body and mind to become Batman, the Dark Knight.

ALFRED PENNYWORTH

Alfred is Bruce Wayne's loyal butler. He knows Bruce is secretly Batman and helps his crime-fighting efforts.

COMMISSIONER GORDON

James Gordon is the Gotham City Police Commissioner. He works with Batman to stop crime in the city.

BATMAN

Batman is an expert martial artist, crime fighter, and inventor. He is known as the World's Greatest Detective.

BATGIRL

Barbara Gordon fights alongside Batman, using high-tech gadgets and martial arts skills. Her father, James Gordon, does not know her secret identity as Batgirl.

THE RIDDLER

Edward Nigma turned his love of puzzles into a life of crime. As the Riddler, this super-villain wields a question-mark cane and asks clever riddles.

Inside Wayne Manor, Gotham City's most powerful people had gathered. Wealthy businessman Bruce Wayne stood before them on a large stage. "Welcome, everyone," Bruce said. "Tonight, I honor one of our finest, Police Commissioner James Gordon." The crowd applauded with excitement as Gordon walked onstage.

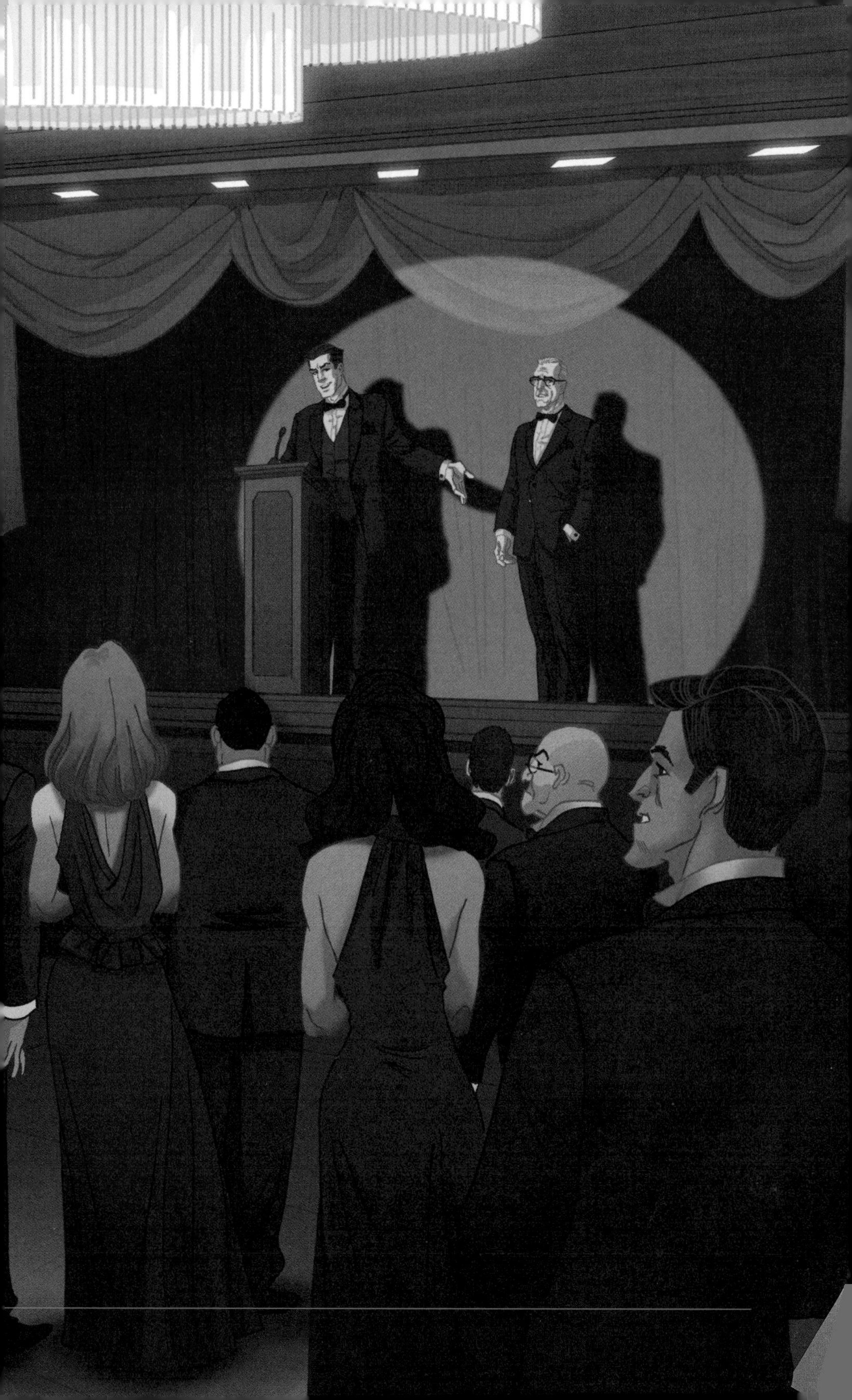

"I'm pleased to present you with a Golden Shield Award," said Bruce, "for cleaning up our city streets." Bruce handed the commissioner his award and shook his hand.

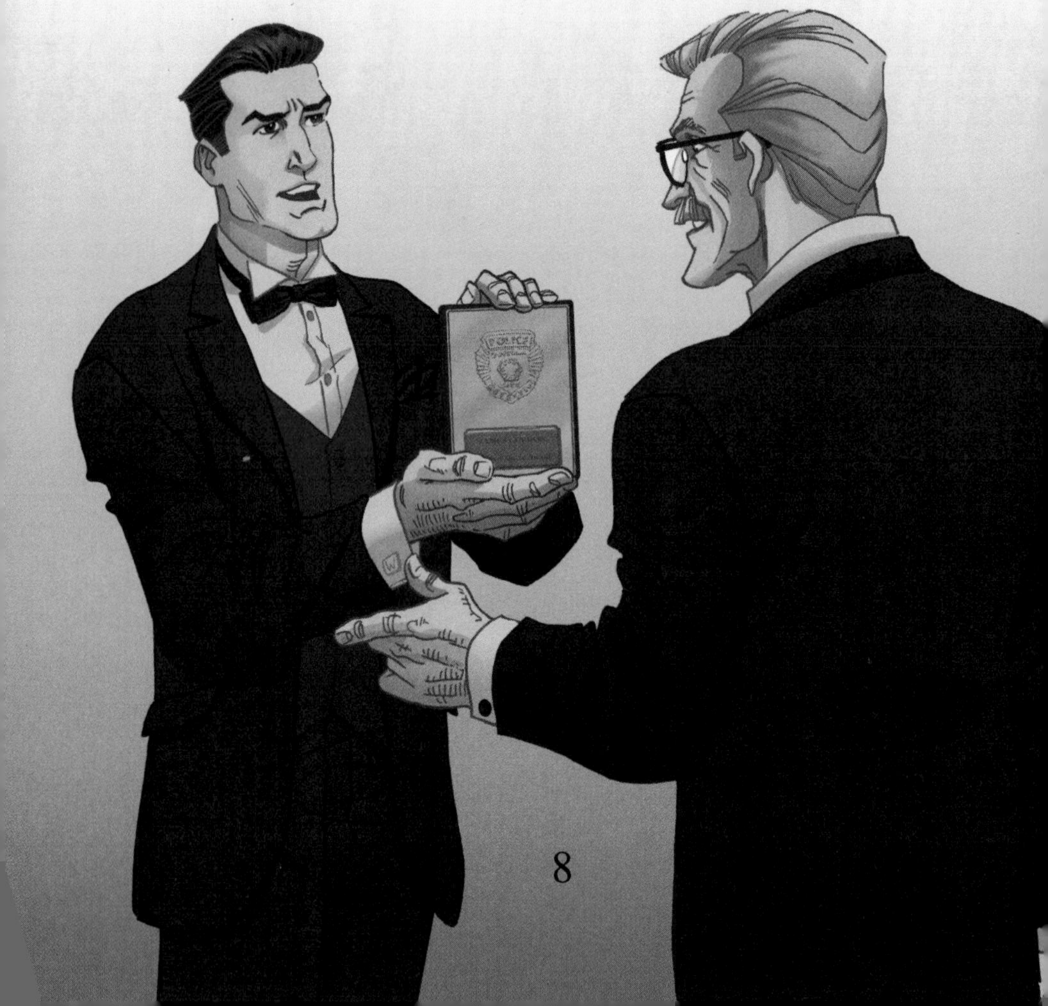

"Thank you, Bruce," said Gordon.

"In fact, I want to thank everyone

for their support, especially my

loving daughter."

He scanned the crowd.

"Where are you, Barbara?"

"Is that a riddle?" asked a voice. Standing in the middle of the room was the city's smartest crook. The Riddler stormed onstage, waving his question-mark cane.

"Where would a teenage girl go?"

the Riddler asked.

"Shopping, of course!"

The villain flicked his wrist, and

green smoke exploded from his cane.

BOOM!

Seconds later, the smoke was gone,

along with Gordon and the Riddler.

As other guests fled to the exits,

Bruce approached his butler,

who knew his secret identity.

"Prepare the Batmobile," said Bruce.

"Have you already solved

the clue, sir?" asked Alfred.

"Of course," Bruce replied.

"The best place to shop is where

you'll find the most sales."

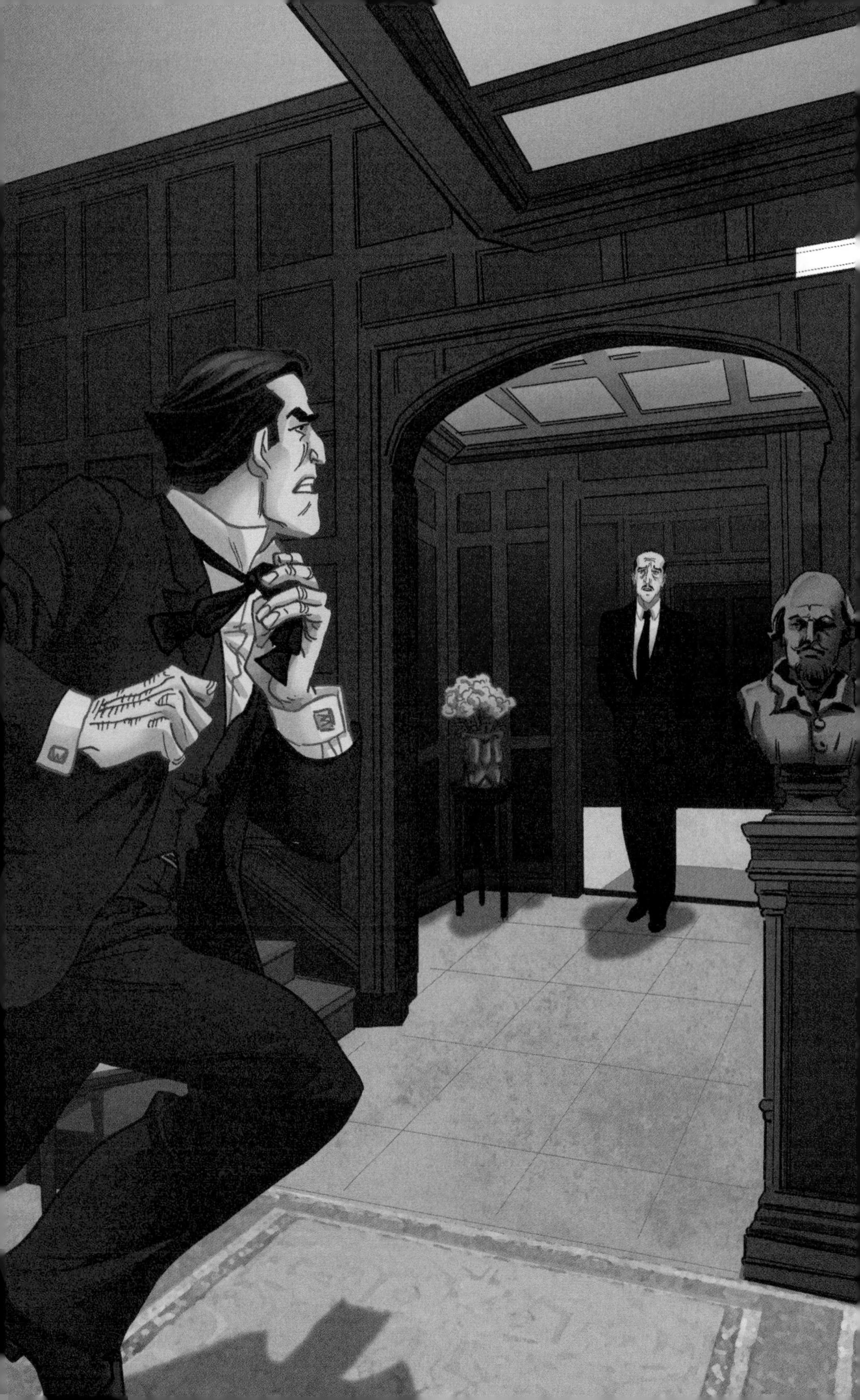

Soon, the Dark Knight arrived at
Gotham Harbor in the Batmobile.
Dozens of sailboats rocked up
and down on the wavy river.
Batman walked along the docks,
searching for another clue.

Suddenly, he spotted a white sail
flapping against the stormy sky.
On it, the Riddler had written a
second message in bold letters:
"Where do fish keep their loot?"

"That riddle's easy," said Batman.

"Fish would keep money

in a riverbank."

The Dark Knight climbed down

to the edge of the Gotham River.

There was the third clue

of the night.

"The more you take," it read,

"the more you leave behind."

"Footprints!" Batman exclaimed.

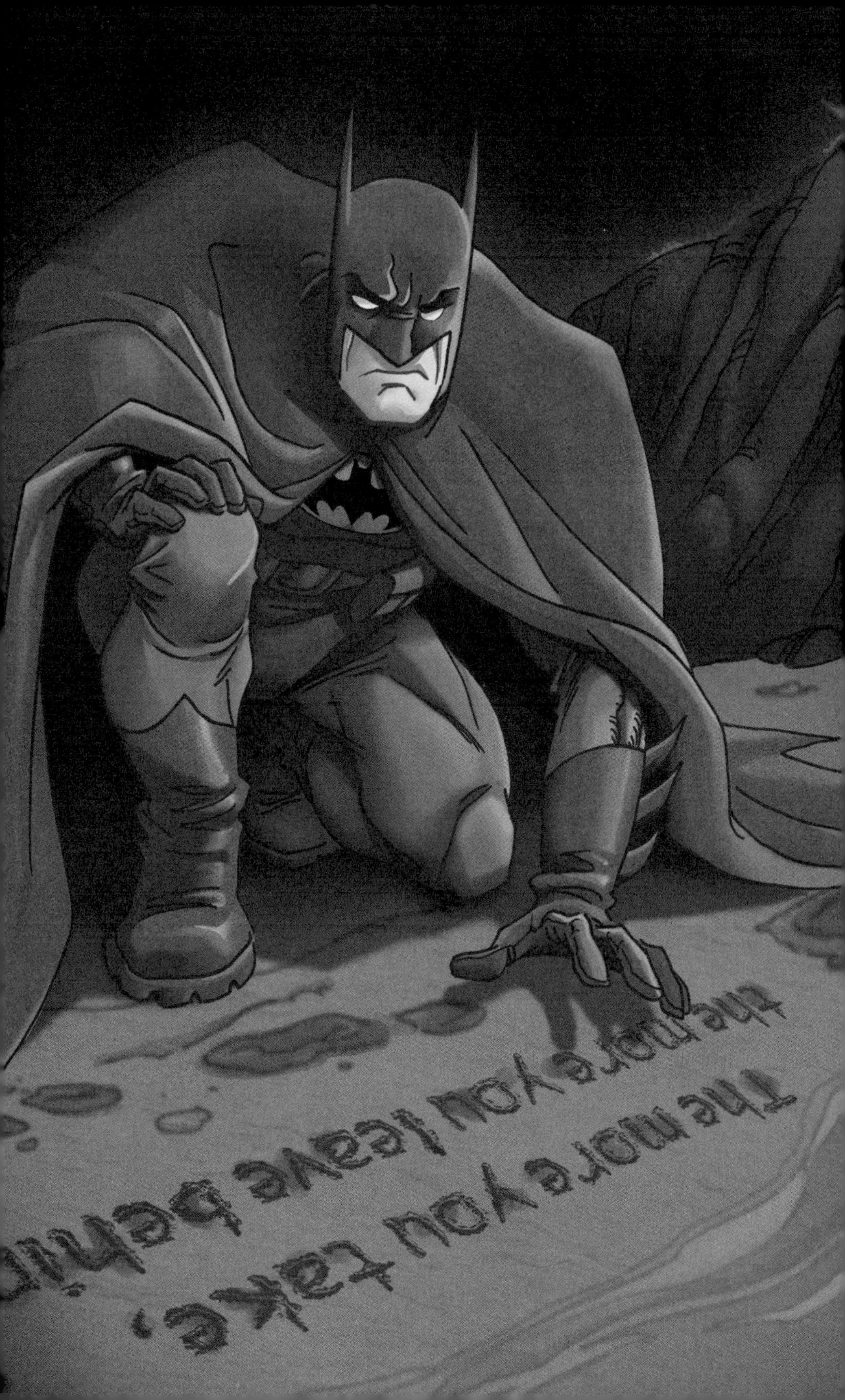
the more you take,
the more you leave behi
the more

Batman followed the trail of
footprints to a large drainpipe.
The hero flipped on his
night-vision goggles.
The pipe led to a dark chamber
with steel doors on all four sides.

Suddenly, the doors slammed shut,
trapping the super hero inside.
Etched on one door was another clue:
"What can you swallow that can
also swallow you?" it read.

"Water," the Dark Knight grumbled. The ankle-deep muck started rising. It quickly reached the hero's neck, threatening to swallow him up.

Just then, another steel door opened.
The water rushed out of the chamber.
Batman slid to a stop at the feet of
Batgirl, his heroic sidekick.
"Good to see you, Barbara," he said,
knowing the teen's secret identity.

"Where were you?" asked Batman.

"I left the party for a moment," Batgirl replied. "When I came back, everyone was gone.

So I tracked my father's phone."

Batgirl spun on her heels.
At her feet, a dark pit dropped
deep into the earth.
"Now let's get to
the bottom of this case," she said.

Batgirl grabbed the grapnel gun
from her Utility Belt.

She fired the gun's metal hook
into the concrete ceiling.

Then she swung over the pit and
began lowering herself down.

The Dark Knight followed.

As the heroes neared the bottom,

a voice echoed in the darkness.

"Well, well," said the Riddler.

"Batman's got brains, after all."

The Riddler stood in the water

at the bottom of the pit.

The commissioner was tied up

on a ledge behind him.

The two heroes hung above the floor.

"When the streets are clean, there's

still scum in the sewers," said Batman.

"Now give us the commissioner."

"Hang in there," joked the Riddler.

"I have one last surprise!"

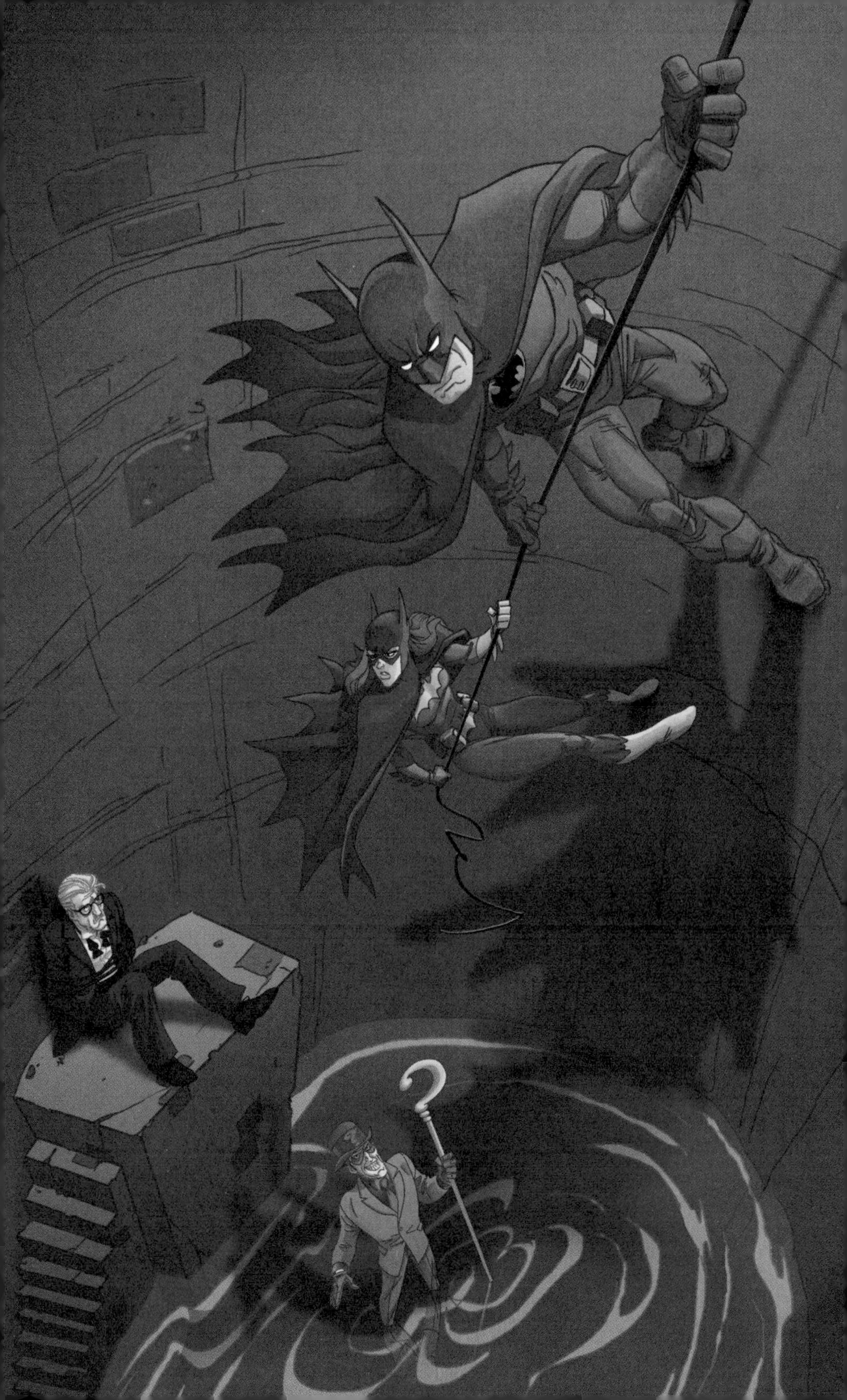

The Riddler raised his cane.

BZZZZ! He fired an electric bolt.

Batman and Batgirl both swung to
the side to avoid the blast.

The bolt struck the water
below their feet.
Electricity jolted everything on
the ground, including the Riddler!
The villain passed out on the floor.

The heroes lowered themselves down.

"The Riddler was right," said Batman.

"That was certainly a surprise."

"Yes, I believe he

even shocked himself," Batgirl joked.

Batman untied the commissioner.

"Thank you, Batman," said Gordon.

Then he turned to Batgirl,

but the teen hero was already gone.

"Where did Batgirl go?" asked Gordon.
Above their heads, Batman heard the
Batcycle speed away from the scene.
"That, Commissioner," he said,
"is a riddle even I can't solve."